Includes Five SAT Words to Know
MEETS STATE AND NATIONAL STANDARDS
RUSSIA
The Great Bear and Its Dramatic History!
IT'S YOUR WORLD
LIVE WORK PLAY LEARN
Where Do You Want to Go?
Hey! It's Saint Basil's cathedral! Do you want to go?
TIME ZONE • CULTURE • CUSTOMS • CLOTHING • HISTORY
FOOD • CULTURE • CUSTOMS • CLOTHING • HISTORY • LANDMARKS
By Carole Marsh

Live • Work • Play • Learn

GALLOPADE INTERNATIONAL

Gallopade International is introducing SAT words that kids need to know in our books. The SAT words in this book have a gray box around them. Students can look up the definitions and increase their vocabulary. Happy Learning!

Gallopade is proud to be a member and supporter of these educational organizations and associations:

Association for the Study of African American Life and History
National Alliance of Black School Educators
American Booksellers Association
American Library Association
International Reading Association
National Association for Gifted Children
The National School Supply and Equipment Association
The National Council for the Social Studies
Museum Store Association
Association of Partners for Public Lands
Association of Booksellers for Children

At the time of publication, all websites referenced in this document were valid. However, due to the changing nature of the Internet, some addresses may change or the content become less relevant.

It's Your World Books

Africa: A Safari Through Its Amazing Nations!

Australia: The Land Down Under for Mates of All Ages!

Canada: The Maple Leaf Melting Pot Country!

China: A Great Wall Runs Thru It!

Egypt: An Ancient Land of Lore; a Modern Land of Oil and More!

France: The Ooh-La-La Country Everyone Loves!

Germany: The Country of Fairytale Castles and Cutting Edge Science!

Greece: A Volcanic Land of Ancient Olympic Origins!

India: Land of Six Senses and Intriguing Mystery!

Italy: The Country of Amazing Fountains and Awesome Arts!

Japan: An Island Country of Endless Intrigue!

Mexico: A Colorful Land of Exotic Culture!

Middle East: Ancient Countries of Current Events Headlines!

Russia: The Great Bear and Its Dramatic History!

South America: A Continent of Countries of Amazing Proportions!

United Kingdom: The Country of Ships, Sealing Wax, Cabbages, and Kings!

Other Carole Marsh Related Titles:

Russian for Kids

Table of Contents

A Letter from the Author

From the desk of CAROLE MARSH

Hey kids,

It's your world! It really, really is!
Of course, you already know that, don't you?
You surf the 'net, listen to satellite radio, watch television shows and movies set all around the globe—kids today are much more "worldly" than in the past and that's a good thing!

Now's a great time to learn something about another country—such as Russia. Why? Because one day, you might actually visit there (if you have not already!). You might go to school there—many colleges have ties with international schools around the globe. You might even go on to work in a foreign country!

Many companies have positions in other countries. Companies are "going global" as fast as they can. They have branch offices, manufacturing plants, and customer service centers scattered around the globe!

So, ready or not: YOU are a Citizen of the World! And you'll want to be a good one. How do you do that? You'll find out everything you can about that country, how it's the same, and how it's different from your own country. What language is spoken there? What customs do the people observe? What foods do they enjoy? What do they do for fun? What has happened in this part of the world, and what is happening there now? It's fun ... and the more you learn, the more you will enjoy whatever global opportunity comes your way!

This book is a good place to start your learning journey—so take advantage of the world— IT'S YOUR WORLD, after all ... and guess what? It's a BIG world, after all!

Happy traveling and learning,

Carole Marsh
Always with passport in hand!

Why Should We Care About Russia?

Russia is the largest country in the world! For most of the 20th century, this beautiful country was mostly off limits to the Western world. With the fall of communism, tourists flock here to see the Hermitage, the Kremlin, Red Square, St. Basil's Cathedral, Lenin's Tomb, the Bolshoi Ballet, and so much more!

Russia is a vibrant nation, active in world affairs. After decades of Communist rule, Russia struggled economically but is quickly gaining a foothold in the global market. It has one of the largest art museums in the world, with over three million pieces of art!

One day, you might visit Russia to see an opera at the Mariinsky Theater, dance for the Bolshoi Ballet, sail on the Black Sea, travel by train from Moscow to Vladivostok, or work for a Russian company. It could happen!

Write home about it!
What will your postcard from Russia say?

Top Fast Russia Facts!

Important facts to remember about the country of Russia:

- Russia is officially called the Federation of Russia.
- Russia used to be known as the Union of Soviet Socialist Republics when it was a communist country. The abbreviated name was the Soviet Union.
- Russia's government today is a federation.
- Russia is a member of the Council of the Baltic Sea States.
- Russia's climate varies from humid continental in Europe, subarctic in Siberia, to tundra climate in the polar region.
- Moscow's Metro was built in the 1930s and is famous for its chandeliers and marble decoration.
- St. Petersburg is sometimes called the "Venice of the North."
- The official language is Russian.
- The currency used is the Russian Federation Ruble.
- The main religion of Russia is Russian Orthodox.

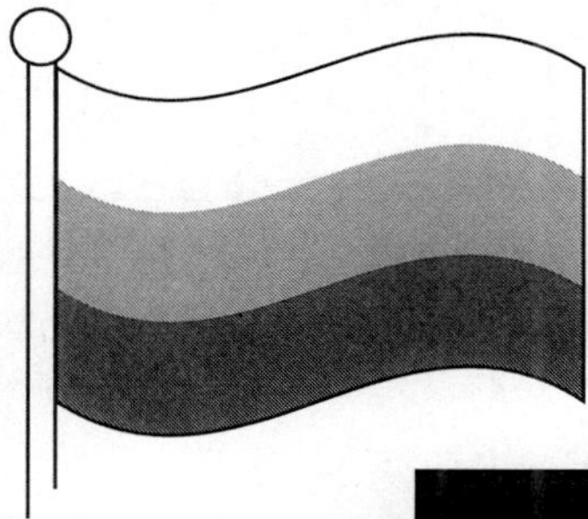

Now, you figure out the rest!

1. This is the Russian ___ ___ ___ ___.

2. This is the national ___ ___ ___ ___ ___ ___ of Russia.

3. Russia's government is a ___ ___ ___ ___ ___ ___ ___ ___ ___ ___.

4. The ___ ___ ___ ___ ___ ___ ___ ___ name of Russia is the Federation of Russia.

5. The ___ ___ ___ ___ ___ ___ ___ ___ ___ ___ of Russia is about 140 million people.

6. The name ___ ___ ___ ___ ___ ___ comes from an ancient group of people called "the Rus."

Where in the World Is Russia?

- Russia is the largest country in the world, located in both the continents of Asia and Europe!
- Just how big is Russia? It covers one-eighth of the earth's surface and has 11 different time zones!
- Moscow is the capital of Russia.
- Russia is surrounded by China, Mongolia, Kazakhstan, Belarus, Ukraine, Latvia, Estonia, and Finland.
- The Volga River is Russia's major river and is the longest in Europe.
- The Ural Mountains separate the European and Asian cultures found in Russia.
- At the end of June, some parts of Russia experience "White Nights." This means the sun never sets!
- Siberia is in the eastern half of Russia and is a frozen tundra climate zone.
- Russia's borders touch two oceans—the Arctic and the Pacific.
- Vladivostok is Russia's largest port city on the Pacific Ocean, connecting to Moscow by the Trans-Siberian Railway.

Do You Know?

1. This river is Russia's major river:
   A. Seine B. Volga C. Thames
2. Russia is bordered by ______ countries.
   A. 8 B. 5 C. 2

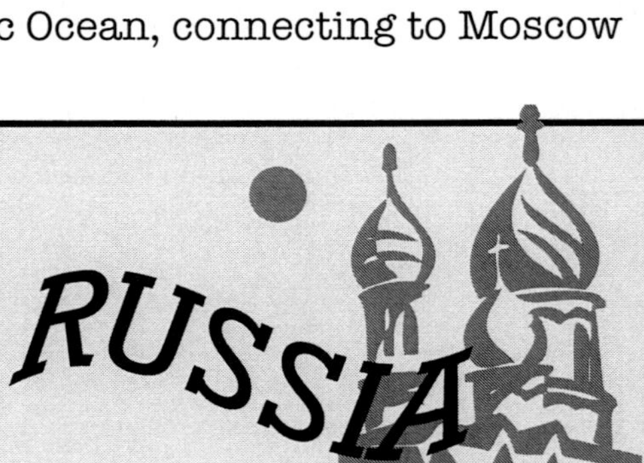

Meet the Czars!

The word "czar" is Russian for "Caesar." A czar was like a king or emperor. Russia's first czar was Ivan the Terrible, who ruled from 1547 to 1584. After Ivan's death, Russia saw many civil wars. In 1613, Michael Romanov became czar. The Romanov Dynasty ruled Russia for 300 years.

Peter the Great changed the face of Russia during his rule in the late 17th and early 18th centuries. After a visit to Western Europe, he realized that Russia needed to modernize. He pushed Russians to adopt Western European ways. He moved the capital to a new city he was building called Saint Petersburg.

Catherine the Great ruled Russia in the late 18th century. She believed that reforms were needed for the serfs. Serfs were peasants who worked the noblemen's lands. They were treated little better than slaves. Although Catherine proposed several reforms, a 1774 rebellion persuaded her that they wouldn't work.

The last Russian czar was Nicholas II. He was an unpopular ruler who was overthrown by the Communist Party. He and his family were arrested and murdered in 1918.

Crosswords!

Use your new knowledge to fill in the crossword puzzle.

Across

2. Catherine the Great proposed ________ for serfs.
3. Nicholas II and his ________ were murdered in 1918.
6. The ________ Dynasty ruled Russia for 300 years.

Down

1. ________ the Great built a new city called Saint Petersburg.
4. Russian ________ were treated little better than slaves.
5. Peter the Great pushed Russia to ________.

The Amazing History of Russia!

Peter the Great

Russia has a long and dramatic history! People have lived in Russia for thousands of years. Slavic peoples from central Asia settled European Russia in the sixth century. Tatars, a warlike people from central Asia, invaded Russia, and ruled for more than 250 years. Eventually the Tatars were overthrown and czars ruled the land for centuries!

The czars expanded Russian territory and united the different Slavic peoples. But they also ruled with an iron fist. They resisted changes that would limit their power. No one suffered more than the serfs—farm laborers who were the property of Russian landowners. They were not freed until 1861.

While Russian peasants suffered, the czar and the nobility lived lives of luxury! Riots and strikes erupted, but were quickly squashed by the czar's military forces. By 1905, Czar Nicholas II was forced to create a legislature called the Duma. However, rebellion did not stop and the Communists overthrew the monarchy. In 1922, Russia ceased to exist and the Union of Soviet Socialist Republics (Soviet Union) was born.

Most people believe that the Communists were just as ruthless as the czars. People were imprisoned or executed. Citizens did not have freedom of speech. Eventually, this system of government broke down. In 1991, the country became Russia once more!

Timeline!

Number these events in the order that they took place, first to last.

_____ Communism is overthrown.

_____ Slavic peoples settle European Russia.

_____ The Soviet Union is created.

_____ Tatars invade Russia.

_____ Serfs are freed.

_____ The Duma is created.

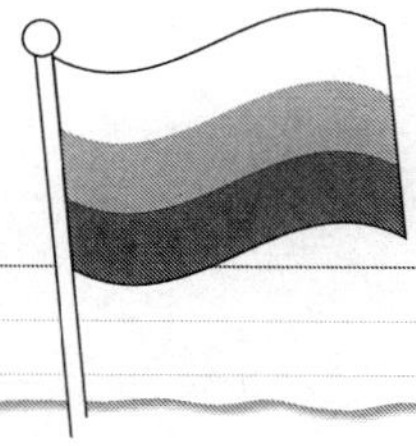

Famous Russian Folks!

Matching!

Match these famous Russian folks with their accomplishments.

_____ 1. Although I was a factory worker from a humble background, I was chosen to participate in the Russian space program. I flew only one flight in space but I made history by becoming the first woman in space!

_____ 2. I was General Secretary of the Communist Party from 1985 to 1991. My efforts to make the political system democratic led to the downfall of communism. My policy of *glasnost* (openness) eventually led to the fall of communism and the Soviet Union. Because of my efforts, I was awarded the Nobel Peace Prize in 1990.

_____ 3. I was born a German princess but became czarina of Russia in 1762. During my reign, I promoted modernization and education. My best legacy is my collection of art, which became the foundation of the famed Hermitage Museum.

_____ 4. I was a famous Russian writer who wrote a collection of fairy-tale stories called *The Malachite Casket*. These tales were based on Ural folklore. The composer Sergei Prokofiev created a ballet based on my book.

_____ 5. I was a composer who lived in the 19th century. Although I composed symphonies, concertos, and operas, I am best known for my ballets. They include *Swan Lake, The Sleeping Beauty,* and *The Nutcracker.*

_____ 6. I am a cosmonaut, which is the Russian version of an astronaut. I have logged more time in space than any other human on Earth. My record is 803 days, nine hours, and 39 minutes!

A. Catherine the Great

B. Valentina Tereshkova

C. Pavel Bazhov

D. Sergei Krikalev

E. Mikhail Gorbachev

F. Peter Tchaikovsky

Guts and Glory Russian Style!

A. He was the first czar of Russia. His name evokes fear and dread. Although he was highly religious, he was also one of the most ruthless and cruel rulers of the country. He was responsible for governmental reform that turned power of the country from the boyars (the nobility) to himself.

____

B. She was the fourth and youngest daughter of Nicholas II and Alexandra. Although she could speak Russian, French, and English fluently, she preferred to climb trees and was considered a tomboy. After the overthrow of her father's regime, she and her family were murdered in 1918. Or was she? There are stories that she was the only one to survive, and some have claimed to be the lost princess.

____

C. This organization was created by Nikita Khrushchev in 1954 to replace the Secret Police. This new organization was responsible for both domestic (at home) and foreign (abroad) spying. Between 1954 and 1991, it acquired vast amounts of money, technical resources, and over 500,000 personnel.

____

D. He was the leader of the Soviet Union from 1929 to 1953. His regime is one of the most terrible in Russian history. It is estimated that between 10 and 20 million Russian citizens died because of his cruel policies. He was one of the "Big Three" leaders of the Allies in World War II—the other two were Franklin D. Roosevelt and Winston Churchill.

____

E. This period of history came as a result of Stalin's post-World War II policies. As Eastern Europe came under Soviet control, communist governments were established in those countries. Western nations, such as the United States and Great Britain, feared this extended Soviet power. The alliance that was created during World War II ended and this period of history began. It would last until 1991.

Mixed Up!
Match the paragraph to the word that the paragraph describes.

JOSEPH STALIN ____

KGB ____

IVAN THE TERRIBLE ____

COLD WAR ____

ANASTASIA ____

Empty Nest

Matryoshka Dolls

Imagine having a toy that was hidden in another toy, which was hidden in another one, and another one, and another one! It's like hiding a treasure or having a secret! That's how *matryoshka* dolls, or nesting dolls, work. Nesting dolls are famous Russian toys. They are made of wood and pull apart in the middle. Inside each doll is a smaller doll. The number of dolls in a set can range from five to thirty!

The word "matryoshka" comes from the name Matryona. This name comes from the Latin word for "mother." Nesting dolls are symbols of motherhood. Many sets have the largest doll representing a mother, with the smaller dolls inside representing her children.

The first nesting dolls were made in a small town called Serviev Posad in 1890. It was a colorful town with a huge marketplace. Many people of different backgrounds attended this market, like merchants, monks, pilgrims, and craftsmen. The first nesting dolls portrayed this colorful life. Dolls included young peasant girls, old religious women, shepherds, old men, and young brides and bridegrooms.

As the popularity of these dolls grew, many more themes were used. Some sets represented an entire family. Some represented Russian nobility, folktale heroes, or historical figures.

Draw It!
Get out your crayons. Create your own set of nesting dolls. How many will be in your set? What is your theme? Be sure to draw each doll a different size.

Peter Carl Fabergé, Master Jeweler!

Have you ever had an Easter egg that was worth millions of dollars? If you owned a Fabergé egg, you would! Peter Carl Fabergé was a jeweler best known for his incredibly decorated eggs. His creations were decorated with metals and jewels rather than crayons and dye. Peter Carl Fabergé was a master craftsman and the official jeweler of the monarchy.

Peter Carl's father was a jeweler. He took over his father's business when he was only 18 years old. He showed his first decorated egg at an exhibition in 1882. People loved it! Czar Alexander III liked the eggs so much that he asked Peter Carl to make a new egg each year for his wife. After the czar died, his son Nicholas II ordered two eggs every year, one for his wife and one for his mother.

Each Fabergé egg was intricately detailed and contained a "surprise." For instance, the "Trans-Siberian" egg was created to celebrate the completion of the Trans-Siberian Railway. Inside was a model train made of silver. The "Cuckoo" egg is decorated with a clock face. When a button on the back is pushed, a small cuckoo rises from the top of the egg, crowing and moving its beak and feathers. When it has finished crowing, the cuckoo slowly descends back into the egg!

Peter Carl's eggs are now housed in museums around the world. They are worth millions of dollars!

Word Play

Use the letters of Peter Carl Fabergé's name to create as many words with three letters or more as you can.

Peter Carl Fabergé

______________	______________	______________
______________	______________	______________
______________	______________	______________
______________	______________	______________
______________	______________	______________
______________	______________	______________

St. Basil's Cathedral, A Site to See!

St. Basil's Cathedral is one of the most beautiful churches in the world! It was built on the edge of Red Square between 1555 and 1561. Some believe that on completion of the church, Czar Ivan the Terrible ordered the architect Postnik Yakovlev to be blinded to prevent him from ever creating anything to rival its beauty again! Ivan named it "The Cathedral of the Intercession of the Virgin on the Moat," after the moat that ran beside the Kremlin. The church was given the nickname "St. Basil's" after the "holy fool" Basil the Blessed. Basil was popular with Ivan after Basil foretold a fire that swept through Moscow that year. Upon his death, Basil was buried in the Trinity Cathedral that stood on this site at the time.

The eight onion dome-topped towers are positioned around a central, ninth spire, forming an eight-point star.

The cathedral is now a museum. One service a year is held in the cathedral, on the Day of Intercession in October.

An architect named Baranovsky once stood on the cathedral's steps and threatened to cut his own throat if Joseph Stalin, a leader of the Soviet Union, tried to destroy the masterpiece.

The interior is a maze of galleries winding from chapel to chapel and level to level via narrow stairways and low arches.

In the 17th century, a bell tower was added.

Create your very own travel pamphlet.
Concentrate on an area that interests you. Perhaps you enjoyed learning about the people. Or maybe it was the monuments that interested you. Fold a piece of paper into three sections. This will give you six areas on which to put information.

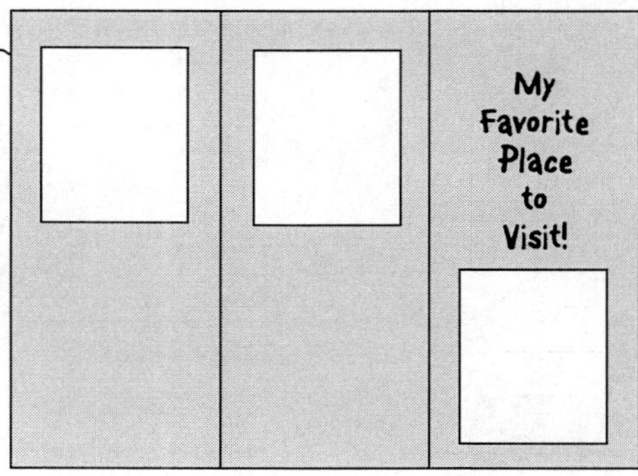

Shake It!

Customs and culture vary widely from country to country. Sometimes they vary in different regions of the same country. Here are custom and cultural differences observed by the Russians!

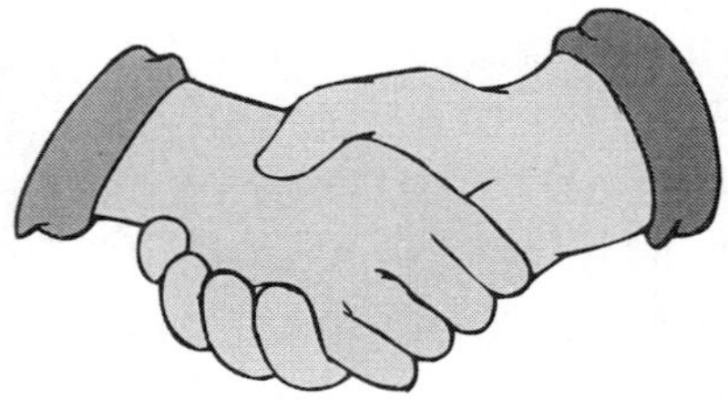

- The handshake is a common greeting. Expect it to be very firm and maybe even a little painful!
- When female friends meet, they kiss each other on the left cheek, the right cheek, and then the left cheek again!
- Middle names are a version of the father's name, with a gender-appropriate ending added. Friends and close acquaintances often refer to each other by their first and middle name.
- When a male guest is invited to dinner, he should bring flowers to the hostess, but never yellow ones!
- Visitors remove their shoes at the front door and are given slippers to wear instead!
- The oldest or most honored guest at the table is served first!
- Asking someone for a favor is a sign that you respect and trust them.

Create your own!

As we have seen, customs and cultural activities can help define who we are. Think about your family and friends and come up with some new customs for everyone to try.

Russia? You Speak Russian?

The official language in Russia is Russian. They use a different alphabet. Their alphabet is the Cyrillic Alphabet.

Match it up!
Below are some common Russian phrases or words. See if you can match them to the English word.

Mahrt	nose
Ahprehl	September
Seentahbr	zero
Deekahbr	March
zahpark	zoo
feelm	movie
nol	April
tree	back
noss	three
speenah	December

Happy Holidays!

There are many special holidays in Russia. **International Women's Day** is celebrated in March. This day honors mothers, grandmothers, wives, and sisters. Women are given flowers and candy. Boys give presents to the girls in their class.

Soldier's Day honors the men of Russia, especially those in the armed forces. It is celebrated in March. Girls give presents to the boys in their class. There is also a fireworks show to celebrate the day.

New Year's Day is the most popular holiday. Russians decorate fir trees and hide presents underneath them for each other. Many people have New Year's parties to celebrate with family and friends. The children wait for Father Frost to bring them presents. He looks a lot like Santa Claus.

Write it down!
Write a letter to Father Frost. Tell him what you would like for New Year's Day.

Russia on the Stage and in the Museums

Music and dance flourish in Russia. It is the birthplace of Mikhail Baryshnikov and home to the Mariinsky Ballet Company and orthodox churches decorated with painted icons.

2.

3.

Notes

1. Ivan the Terrible erected St. Basil's Cathedral with its painted onion domes in 1560.
2. The Mariinsky Theatre became the finest music and ballet venue of late 19th century Russia.
3. The Theotokos of Vladimir is the world's most beloved icon of the Virgin Mary in the world.
4. Tchaikovsky's *Nutcracker* ballet, first performed in St. Petersburg in 1892, never gained popularity in Russia.
5. Each character in Sergei Prokofiev's musical story *Peter and the Wolf* is represented by a different instrument or group of instruments.

1.

5.

4.

What's for Dinner?

The Russian diet has a wide variety of foods. The big meal of the day is enjoyed around 1:00 P.M. Take a look below at some foods you may find in Russia.

Borscht is a soup made of beets and served with sour cream on top.

Pirozhok is a small pie, either fried or baked, and filled with meat, fish, or potatoes.

Caviar is a very expensive food and is considered a delicacy. It is the eggs of a fish called sturgeon.

Blini are Russian pancakes—yummy!

RECIPE

Always ask an adult for help when cooking!

Russian Tea Cakes

INGREDIENTS

1 cup butter, room temperature
1/2 cup confectioners' sugar
2 1/4 cups sifted flour
1 teaspoon vanilla
3/4 cup finely chopped walnuts or pecans
confectioners' sugar for rolling

mmmmmmm...this was good!

DIRECTIONS

Preheat the oven to 400°F.
Cream the butter, adding sugar gradually until light and fluffy.
Stir in flour, vanilla, and walnuts or pecans.
Roll between hands into 1-inch balls. Place on an ungreased baking sheet.
Bake for 12 to 14 minutes.
Using pot holders, remove the cakes from the oven.
While still warm, roll in confectioners' sugar. Place on a cooling rack to cool.

A Sport You Can Flip For!

Gymnastics is a very popular sport in Russia! Gymnasts need to be strong, flexible, agile, and coordinated. The best known kind of gymnastics is Artistic Gymnastics. If you watched the last Olympic Games, you saw women compete in four different events—uneven parallel bars, balance beam, vault, and floor exercise. Men's events include high bar, parallel bars, pommel horse, rings, vault, and floor exercise. Each athlete is judged and given a score. Russia has dominated the sport for many years and is still a powerhouse in gymnastics!

Figure it out!

Figure out the answers to these questions about gymnastics.

Gymnastics is a great way to improve balance and strength!

1. After Olga competes in all of her events, she has a combined score of 39.86 and is in the lead for a gold medal. Nadia has one more event to go and currently has a score of 31.14. What score must she earn on her last event to win the gold?

____

2. There are only 65 days left until the next big competition for the Russian gymnastics team! If today is April 12th, what day is the competition? (Hint: Today should be counted as Day 1!)

____

Mighty Moscow!

How old is your town? If you lived in Moscow, you'd be able to boast that yours is at least 3,000 years old!

Moscow became a relatively large city in the 14th and 15th centuries. With its growing population and industries, it was becoming the place to go in Russia! Moscow became the capital of Russia in 1480. It was during this time that the fortress called the Kremlin was built to defend the city.

In 1812, Napoleon marched on Moscow to capture it. He understood that the city was the heart of the Russian people. Before Napoleon could enter the city, the Muscovites burned the city! There was little for Napoleon to capture! Hunger forced him to withdraw and Moscow was liberated.

Moscow is the birthplace of many famous artists, writers, and painters. The city is full of history, and there are fun things to do if you visit. The Moscow Zoo has over 5,000 rare and exotic animals and birds. The Cosmonaut Museum celebrates the achievements of Russians in space—after all, they were the first ones to go there! And don't forget to ride the roller coasters at Gorky Park, Moscow's most famous funfair!

Real or Fiction?
Are these places in America or Russia? List them under the proper column.

Disney World, Cosmonaut Museum, Moscow Zoo, San Diego Zoo, Kennedy Space Center, Gorky Park, Moscow, New York City

America	Russia

Russia Did It First!

What a Great View!
Yuri Gagarin was the first human to go into space and orbit the earth on April 12th, 1961.

Goal!
Viktor Nechaev, in 1982, was allowed to leave the USSR to be with his American wife. He played three games for the Los Angeles Kings and became the first Soviet citizen to play in the National Hockey League.

Checkmate!
From 1948 to 1972, Russia dominated the world of competitive chess. Russian Garry Kasparov is still considered the best chess player of all time.

Word Fun!

This is fun to do with someone else. Ask a friend for words to substitute for the blanks in the story. Their word substitutions will have a humorous effect when the resulting story is then read aloud.

I want to be the first person to ______________ (ACTION VERB)

across ______________ (COUNTRY)! I've been training for this

since ______________ (MONTH). I'm in ______________ (ADJECTIVE) shape.

My ______________ (ADJECTIVE) adventure will begin on

______________ (FAVORITE HOLIDAY). I will be hard to miss;

I'll be the one wearing a ______________ (COLOR)

______________ (ARTICLE OF CLOTHING) and a pair of matching

______________ (FOOTWEAR). My faithful friends

______________ (FAMOUS ATHLETE) and

______________ (CARTOON CHARACTER) will be there to cheer for me.

I'm bringing my ______________ (NOUN) along for good luck.

I'm confident I'll be the first!

Under Pressure!
The first full pressure suit was designed by engineer Evgeniy Chertanovskiy in Leningrad in 1931. This type of suit helps pilots breathe when flying at high altitudes.

I Saw It on TV!
Russian inventor Vladimir Zworykin invented the cathode-ray tube called the kinescope in 1929. The kinescope tube made the electronic transmission of pictures possible, which we now know as television.

Before the Boom!
Alexander Stepanovich Popov invented the lightning detector. A ground-based version of this device is used by the National Weather Service to help detect storms.

That's One Big Cat!

Siberian Tiger

Did you know that the largest tiger in the world is found in Russia? It is the Siberian tiger! These "big cats" live in eastern Russia's forests, although some can be found in North Korea and China. Siberian tigers are an endangered species. This means that there are not many of them, and they could become extinct. There are only about 400 to 500 Siberian tigers left in the wild.

The Siberian tiger is unique. Its fur is orange and black striped, which makes good camouflage for the forest! Tigers like to live in areas with a lot of plant life so they can sneak up on their prey! Did you know that no two tigers have exactly the same stripes? Their stripes are sort of like "tiger fingerprints"!

Siberian tigers can grow up to 11 feet long and weigh more than 650 pounds! Female tigers have litters of two to six cubs and raise them without the male. Cubs cannot hunt until they are 18 months old. That's why they usually stay with their mothers for two to three years.

Poachers hunt Siberian tigers for their fur. In China, poachers also sell skin and body parts to make medicines. Many conservation groups have set up programs to help keep the magnificent Siberian tigers alive!

Word Fun!

You are a reporter covering the story of poaching of the Siberian Tiger. What questions would you ask?

Example: How do poachers find the tigers they are hunting?

1. ____?
2. ____?
3. ____?
4. ____?
5. ____?

Mr. Gorbachev, Tear Down This Wall!

Did you know that no shots were fired during the Cold War? This was a time in history when democracy and communism were battling to gain control. The Soviet Union was spreading communism, while the United States tried to spread democracy. The best example of these hostilities can be found in the city of Berlin, Germany.

Berlin was divided into East Berlin and West Berlin, even though the city was located in East Germany. The people of East Germany lived under a communist government. They were not free, like the people in West Germany.

The Berlin Wall Just Before Being Torn Down

Many East Berliners fled to West Berlin—as many as 1,500 per day! In 1961, the East Germans built a wall in the middle of Berlin to keep their citizens from leaving. It was made of barbed wire and concrete. Armed guards were ordered to shoot escapees on sight. The Berlin Wall became a hated symbol of the Cold War.

Eventually, communism began to fail in the east. Mikhail Gorbachev, the leader of the Soviet Union, visited Berlin in 1987. U.S. President Ronald Reagan was also there. He demanded, "Mr. Gorbachev, tear down this wall!"

In November of 1989, the East Germans opened the border between East and West Berlin for private family trips. Thousands of people showed up at the wall! There was mass confusion! The guards, not knowing what to do, let the people through. The wall had come down!

Revealing Answer!

Follow the instructions to reveal the nickname of a famous checkpoint, or crossing point, between East and West Berlin during the Cold War.

1. Cross off the first and last letters.
2. Cross off any letter "O."
3. Cross off the letter that represents the Roman numeral 10.
4. Cross off the first and second "E"s from the left.
5. Cross off the fifth letter from the right.
6. Cross off the seventh and last letters of the alphabet.

D E C O G H A E X R Z L X W I O E K

You Say You Want a Revolution...

Nicholas II

The American Revolution was fought because the colonists were unhappy with their king. Did you know that the Russian Revolution was fought for the same reason? Nicholas II was the last czar of Russia. His family ruled the country for more than 300 years. But many Russians were unhappy with Nicholas. By the end of Nicholas' reign, Russia was fighting in World War I and losing to Germany. Many soldiers were rationed to just one bullet a day! People did not have enough food. Citizens grew angry! Finally, Nicholas was forced to give up his throne. In March 1917, the Duma (legislature) took control.

However, the Duma had the same problems as Nicholas—military defeats and severe food shortages. The people desperately wanted a change. The Bolshevik Party promised that change and overthrew the government in November 1917. They quickly signed a peace treaty with Germany and withdrew from the war.

The Bolsheviks, who became the Communist Party, were led by Vladimir Lenin. Lenin declared that all property belonged to the communist government. He imprisoned people who didn't agree with him or were a danger to him. Czar Nicholas II, Czarina Alexandra, and their five children were arrested and imprisoned.

Opposition forces (called the White Army) fought the communists (called the Red Army) in a civil war that lasted for three years. In the end, the communist government won and established the Soviet Union in 1922.

Cross It Off!

Many Russian military parades have taken place in this vast meeting place in Moscow. Starting with the first letter, cross off every other letter to reveal the English translation of its name, *Krasnaya Ploschad*.

SRWERDCSBQVUNAJRNET

____

Majestic Peterhof!

Picture yourself cutting through the Baltic Sea on a fast boat. Suddenly, a huge palace looms before you! The palace and park at Peterhof is one of the most famous and popular attractions in St. Petersburg. It is often referred to as "the Russian Versailles," but many consider it to be more majestic and spectacular than its sister palace in France.

The Grand Cascade at Peterhof

Peterhof (called Petrodvorets in Russian) was built by Peter the Great. He wanted something large and majestic for his namesake city. He used the palace at Versailles as his model. The Grand Palace has a magnificent staircase, golden statues, and elegant furniture fit for royalty.

The surrounding grounds are gorgeous, featuring a fabulous system of more than 100 fountains. The most remarkable of these fountains are the Grand Cascade and the Samson Fountain. The fountains are a favorite with kids as they try to guess which one will go off next! The park also includes beautifully groomed gardens and a grotto that looks out over the Baltic Sea.

During World War II, German troops greatly damaged Peterhof. However, after the war, it was one of the first estates to be restored. Thanks to the work of engineers and volunteers, we can appreciate and enjoy Peterhof today!

True or False?

Read the statements below. Write T if the statement is true, and F if it is false.

____ 1. Peterhof is a palace and park in Russia.

____ 2. Peterhof is located along the Mediterranean Sea.

____ 3. A French palace was the model for Peterhof.

____ 4. There are more than 100 fountains on the grounds of Peterhof.

____ 5. Japanese bombs destroyed Peterhof during World War II.

____ 6. Peterhof was built by the Russian czar Ivan the Terrible.

Russian Fashion

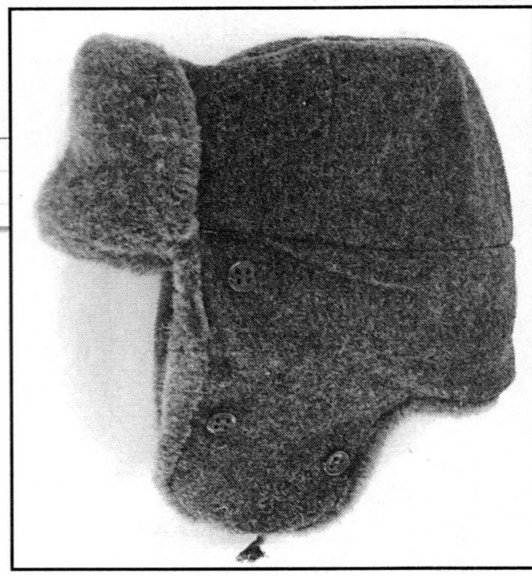

Ushanka

When you think of Russian fashion, what comes to mind? Well, shorts and flip-flops are definitely out, as Russia is a very cold country. How about a hat? The *ushanka* is a kind of hat found in Russia. It is such a popular design that you can find it in just about any cold weather country in the world!

The ushanka is a Russian fur hat with ear flaps. The flaps can either be tied on top of the head (pulling the flaps up the side of the hat) or under the chin (bringing the flaps down over the ears). However, this was not a Russian invention. The Finnish people came up with the design first.

Ushankas are made of sheepskin, rabbit fur, muskrat fur, or artificial fur. They are a common part of the winter uniforms of Russian police forces and the military. However, they are also used by civilians. With the fall of the Soviet Union in 1991, these warm hats entered the American market to stay!

Dress Up!

Help Christina get dressed for her tour of Russia! Here are some traditional Russian costumes. Choose which outfit she'll wear. Color the clothing, and draw a line from the piece of clothing to Christina or cut the clothing out and dress her up!

Assorted Architecture!

Figure it out!

Use the following clues to figure out the name of this famous building in St. Petersburg, Russia.

- Construction of this building lasted from 1883 to 1907.
- It is better known as the "Church of the Spilled Blood."
- It was built on the spot where Czar Alexander II was assassinated.
- This building is very Russian in appearance, but its main architect was not Russian.
- After World War II, it was used as a warehouse.
- The most impressive part of this building is the extravagant shrine to Alexander II. It is decorated with beautiful mosaics and carved stone.

2.

4.

6.

1.

3.

5.

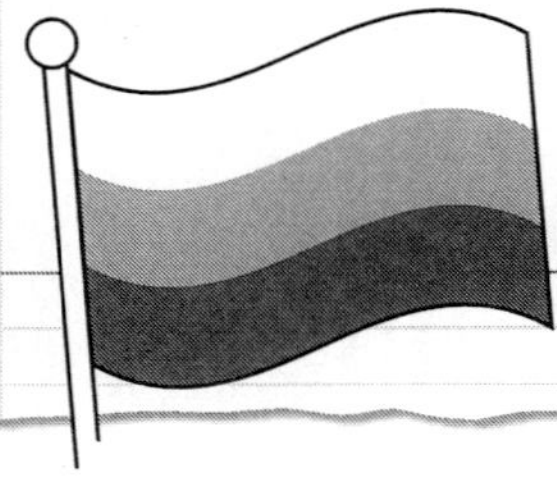

As They Say in Russia...

Here are a few Russian words you may already know. Why? Because we use them as "English" words all the time!

balalaika: a Russian musical instrument with a triangular body and three strings

borscht: a beet soup served hot or cold

cosmonaut: a Russian or Soviet astronaut

gulag: a forced labor camp or prison

Kremlin: the citadel of Moscow that houses the Russian government

mammoth: huge

Molotov cocktail: a crude bomb made with a bottle, a wick, and flammable liquid

ruble: a Russian unit of currency

sable: a carnivorous mammal of the weasel family found in northern Asia

samovar: a metal urn with a spigot used to serve tea or hot water

Sputnik: a Russian satellite

steppe: a vast, semiarid, grass-covered plain

vodka: an alcoholic liquor

____

____

____

____

Further Resources

U.S. Embassy in Moscow, Russia
Bolshoy Deviatinsky Pereulok No. 8
Moscow 121099, Russian Federation
Phone: +7 (495) 728-5000
Fax: +7 (495) 728-5090

United Nations
2 United Nations Plaza
New York, NY 10017

Russian National Tourist Office
5/10 Chistoprudni Blvd., Suite 214
Moscow, Russia 109391

Russian Travel Guide–St. Petersburg
19 Michurinskaya St.
Saint Petersburg, Russia 197046
info@visitrussia.com

Interesting Websites

http://www.russia-travel.com/

http://www.moscow-landmarks.com/

http://www.saint-petersburg.com/

http://www.visitrussia.com

Answer Key

Page 7 1. flag 2. symbol 3. federation 4. official 5. population 6. Russia

Page 8 1. B 2. A

Page 9

Page 10 6, 1, 5, 2, 3, 4

Page 11 1. B 2. E 3. A 4. C 5. F 6. D

Page 12 A. Ivan the Terrible B. Anastasia C. KGB D. Joseph Stalin E. Cold War

Page 17

Mahrt	March
Ahprehl	April
Seentahbr	September
Deekahbr	December
zahpark	zoo
feelm	movie
nol	zero
tree	three
noss	nose
speenah	back

Page 21
1. 8.73
2. June 15th

Page 22

American - Disney World, San Diego Zoo, Kennedy Space Center, New York City

Russian - Cosmonaut Museum, Moscow Zoo, Gorky Park, Moscow,

Page 25 Charlie

Page 26 Red Square

Page 27
1. T
2. F
3. T
4. T
5. F
6. F

Page 29 Church of the Resurrection of Jesus Christ